HOW THE WIZARD CAME TO THE CHERRYTHORPE

Patrick Muñoz

BAMBOO DART PRESS

LOS ANGELES † NEW YORK † LONDON † MELBOURNE

How the Wizard Came to the Cherrythorpe by Patrick Muñoz

978-1-962316-07-1   Paperback

978-1-962316-08-8   Ebook

Cover art by Dennis Callaci

Layout and design by Mark Givens

For information:

Bamboo Dart Press

chapbooks@bamboodartpress.com

Bamboo Dart Press 053

SHRiMPER

www.pelekinesis.com   www.bamboodartpress.com   www.shrimperrecords.com

For Cameron, who said that if I read for ten more years, I could be a good writer.

I

That fall Thomas came to the barony, wearing the mantle of a wizard. The locals inclined to suspicion of itinerant sorts, but they were reluctant to kick him on his way, being dazzled in spite of themselves by the colors of that mantle. A blue crown, red breast, and green wings, with the hues all bled together: it was bad luck to bother a magic man. Still they wouldn't suffer him too near the less eccentric stock in town, and so he set himself up out beyond the palisade, against the wall ringing the threshing floor, to hawk spikenard oil and mustard aphrodisiac.

They let him eat from the poor-due pears at the fringe of the baron's orchard, hoping he would move on without a fuss, but a week and a half on he was still sleeping in the grass. By then no one could stop the kids in town from being curious enough to bother him, and some of them crept up onto the wall to drop little stones and pits on his head before giggling wildly and ducking back behind.

Thomas didn't chase them to hit them with their own pellets, or yell after them, or bother to stop being an easy target slumped at the foot of the wall – he scooped up the stones and pits again, to toss them back over. Some of the kids were happy to reuse them, and others were too puzzled to respond, and let him alone when their puzzlement gave way to boredom. Among those that stayed playing on the threshing floor until sunset was Mary, who stopped on her way back to town and stood in the grass to stare at Thomas as he sat smoking in the westering light.

"Do some magic," she said.

"Well, alright, lass, if that's what you want," Thomas said.

Thomas reached into his satchel, bleached dry and stained green with exposure, and rummaged around for some moments – there was the sound of clinking glass, and liquid in motion, as the smoke from the pipe between his teeth curled up above his hood, to be dispersed by the breeze.

"Here," he said, pulling out a little wooden jewelry box, and a copper bowl of the sort the brothers used for begging. He filled the bowl with water, placed it on the ground, stood up, and came towards Mary, the box still in hand.

"Alright, now watch this," Thomas said, and he slid open the box's lid to reveal behind the chipped paint a collection of pale granules, the largest no bigger than half a pinky fingernail.

"What are they?" Mary asked. She brushed her hair out of her eyes when the wind blew it there. Thomas held a finger in the air signaling for her patience, and stayed still for a minute until the breeze became still with him. Then he nodded, pinched one of the granules between his thumb and forefinger, and deftly let it fly from his hand.

It landed in the bowl, and there was the sound of sizzling that congealed into a whip crack. Mary started, then gasped as a little conflagration lit up the air, a beacon shooting skyward; it made the vicinity like daylight, and threw their shadows behind them over the grass. It was gone as soon as it appeared, leaving a smell of ash and pepper. The water in the bowl rippled, and smoke rose over its rim in mimicry of the smoke from Thomas' pipe. In a moment, the breeze began again.

The next day Thomas was beset by children, all clamoring for his attention and asking for another demonstration. Mary was indignant, insisting she hadn't made it up, but Thomas shrugged and said magic wasn't a toy – it wasn't meant to be used for the entertainment of any onlooker who took the fancy. They gathered around him, hemming him to the wall in a semicircle, as he sat carving the final touches on a little wooden horse in mid-gallop. "What does it do?" another girl asked, pointing to it a little too quickly, in the way children do.

"Nothing, it's just a little knickknack," Thomas said, running his thumb over the mane. "Why, do you want it?" The girl's eyes were wide, and so Thomas laughed and tossed it to her. She caught it and laughed herself, and at once began running her thumb over its coat, and looking intently at its large eyes.

"Where'd you come from?" a boy asked him.

"From the Jasmine," Thomas said, "on a sick wind that smelled of flowers." And this delighted them all, as it was the sort of thing, they knew, that wizards said.

They were soon asking for stories, and so Thomas obliged them. He said that a giant seahorse named Horschell built the jetty at Heighnsing Head, and that she was friends with the giant who built the lighthouse, and that on the equinox you could see her silhouette beneath the water from the shore. It was exhausting, Thomas thought, to have people that wanted to listen to you.

This sort of thing went on for some days, and their parents told the kids once, twice, and a million times to stop bothering about such balderdash, and to get back home or they'd get a thrashing, and so on. But they said it with a sideways glance, not being entirely sure that the words of a wizard should ever be discounted, and they sometimes crossed themselves after speaking ill of Thomas.

That was how the people got used to him, and as no one has the energy to maintain a suspicion of what does them no bodily harm, they were quick in becoming lax about his presence. He was soon in the town square giving fortunes, and divining the location of sunken treasure in the hills with a peepstone. When a passerby asked him why, if he knew where all these nuggets of gold and dragons' teeth were hidden in the earth, he did not dig them up himself, and so make his own fortune instead of bothering other people with theirs, Thomas replied that this really was a crass thing to say – did this upstart ever hear of a wizard doing such a thing in the scriptures, and so forth? Well, his accuser admitted that he did not know precisely what the scriptures said that wizards got up to or had gotten up to. Thomas shook his head, saying, "Incredible that you admit your own utter ignorance, after you chastise me for something you know nothing about." And the onlookers thought this an exceedingly perspicacious reply.

These antics got to annoying the grandfather from the farm on the Jansen hill, who in his age had himself taken to the use of seeing stones, and made a modest sum recovering lost objects for his countrymen. Thomas suspected that the reason he went from home to home asking if anyone needed anything found (whether that be a whetstone or a button, or something less tangible, like a 'way,' which was always being lost in the old man's estimation) was because he was getting sentimental, and wasn't sure how to have company once his working days were done. Thomas happened to know that the elder Jansen's peepstones were fraudulent – they were just rocks, after all – but he liked the man for his gumption, and on being told off by him, Thomas apologized and said that he wouldn't have thought to offer his services as a treasure-finder had he known another was in town. It was unwise to have multiples in one place, and as with most things, where two were in competition, the older was likely the better.

And so he fell into his role as an inconstant journeyman, with a knack for metal, but not much for labor so long as starvation was kept at bay. He charmed the Meikeljohns by mending a plow for them, and so was able to sleep in the storeroom by their smithy, and soon he was blessing their weapons. But the public interest in magic waned before long, and those not taken with Thomas started to resent the nuisance of having to see a vagrant around. They noted he was a pretentious wastrel, who whiled away the goodwill of the barony dicing with the men at the gate-house, and selling them moonshine. It was unwise for Thomas to have associated with the guards; during planting season for the winter wheat, hatred for professional soldiers ran high, since it was asked why there should be men sitting within the palisade polishing themselves, when they could be out in the field. It was only natural that this question should be extended to Thomas, and being used to such critique, he began to wonder whether there were wisdom in staying any longer.

At length the locals became fussy, and requested that he justify his existence. Thomas informed them that he could see more in his mind's eye than just baubles: he could see, for instance, where a remnant band of Jordan's loyalists were headquartered, in the woods three or so miles north of the valley on the Hellebore's frontier. They were living off the king's venison, he thought, and no doubt their intentions were violent, or at least irreligious. The baron sequestered in his keep was a melancholy and superstitious sort, prone to omens and guesses, and so scouts were sent to where the scryer pointed them – and there the loyalists were, not quite as Thomas had described them, but close enough that there was no more question of driving the man out of town. And good riddance, Thomas thought, when the soldiers returned one afternoon with their spears bloodied.

That was how, for a brief time, Thomas lived in peace, at the barony in the Hellebore, and how for that time, he became a fixture within the palisade by the woods. He still sat by the threshing floor wall when the opportunity presented itself, but more often he was against the wall of the town, within rather than without, selling whatever came out of his head or his satchel, thinking of the Jasmine and wishing that he had somewhere to go.

In the bright chill of early winter, Thomas sat by the cornerstone of the church, listening to the mockingbirds in the steeple. He could see his breath just vaguely, out of his mouth but not out of his nostrils, and he flexed his fingers hard against his palms every few minutes. In that dull reverie, something came to him as he prayed: from the other side of the inner wall, out through the gatehouse, it approached slowly, tramping across the ground at a steady pace, out of earshot at first, but coming in clearer by the second, until there was the sound of feet on grass, then dirt, then cobbles, and Thomas looked up.

There were three men there, with ornamented weapons – they glinted in the sunlight at their backs, and made Thomas blink. The man in the middle, whose spear had a tassel hung off the point, and whose livery was distinguished by a silver patch on the breast, detached himself from the others, and stood just a few feet before Thomas, so that a shadow was cast over him and the stone of the church wall.

"Wizard," the man said.

"Yes?"

"The baron has called for you at the estate."

And so Thomas picked himself up, and dusted off his trousers, and followed the soldiers back the way they'd come, past the gatehouse of the inner wall, into the estate in the shadow of the motte, where the baron's keep stood.

II

Beyond the gate, the town's bustle drifted out of hearing, and Thomas laid eyes on that portion of the Hellebore he had never seen before: the silent estate past the inner wall had an elevation to it, though its people were no fairer, and it structures no grander. Yet the motte was closer here, just beyond the further inmost wall, and from it indeed rose the grandest structure Thomas had ever seen. The fort's presence was indelible now, and its vicinity made it loom always in the corner of one's eye, and always up above, as if it were founded on the air. The buildings lining the wall through which Thomas and the soldiers passed faced inward in unison, all turned toward the motte and its crowning edifice, watching the battlements in hushed reverence.

They headed west past the armory and the dovecote, to the far end of the grounds. There the woods spilled over the wall, so that a patch of forest lay within the barony grounds, as if it pained the Hellebore's forebears so greatly to part from the touch of their ancient love that they ran the boundary of their fastness through her fingertip. Or again, those old Hellebore builders, their palms still smelling of dirt and flower petals, raised their wall flirtatiously, to be near her, yet with a curtain to fend her off, and the unborn trees, sensing men, had sprung up inside the boundary for a rendezvous. Or again, the Hellebore and the forest had always existed, stone and wood, before the Lord and before the Cow, and had crept toward each other in the mythic ink, until at their meeting the world sprang into being, the wall set between them, but imprecisely, each one admitting a piece of the other.

And within the barony's side of the border there ran another, lesser wall, this one painted with sedges and daffodils, that girdled these errant trees against that border and parted them from the rest of the grounds; they were thus penned into a wild park, a piece of the forest cut off from its kin and kept fast for the pleasure of the Hellebore. There the elms grew in a walled wood, secreted against both the out and the in sides, and made a silent, shaded place.

A pair of nervous men flanked the gate into that enclosure, and as Thomas and company approached, the two undistinguished men in their party fell off to join them. Their captain, that third man with his silver patch, the tassel still bobbing off the tip of his spear, motioned to Thomas to follow, and pressed his way through a little man-size door set within the broader frame of the gate. The two of them entered among the standing sentinels in the white-gray silence, and the blue-gray sky peeked through the crosshatched mess of branches. "Come on, then," the captain said, motioning up along a path set between two rows of stones, thinly visible under the powder snow.

They walked on as the elms watched them, and in only a minute they came upon the clearing at the center of the enclosure, where there stood a muted cottage, grim yet inviting, as if the planks of its cruck acknowledged the cold with the promise to keep it at bay. By the doorframe stood an older man, a cap in his hands, who shivered slightly; on approaching, it was clear he had been weeping. As the guard entered, Thomas followed, nodding to the man, and getting no response.

Inside the cottage there sat another man at a table in the center of the room, and off to the right of the entrance, on the floor and huddled back to the wall, sat a woman in some distress, who alternated between holding her knees and pressing her loose-hanging hair back over her head and behind her ears. The man at the table, whose boyish face had been shaped by a lifetime of contradictory pressures into a round equilibrium, introduced himself to Thomas as the baron's chamberlain.

"Where's the baron? Ought I to speak to him?" Thomas asked.

"You'll speak to me," the chamberlain said. "There is a matter concerning my lord's son. You're here in the paradise because the matter is a delicate one, and I require your oath that you'll be discreet about the baron's affairs before I speak to you any further."

Thomas shrugged his shoulders easily. "Yes, I swear," he said.

There was some ice in the air at that reply, and it congealed about Thomas, but the chamberlain looked him over and continued. "In knowing what I'm to tell you, you'd join only the baron, I myself, the head groom–" he pointed towards the outside, where the man stood by the door, "–and the captain of the guard." His eyes flicked to the corner of the room where the disheveled woman sat breathing heavily. "And Rebekah," he said. Thomas' instinct for flight had begun to assert itself; the counting of these figures seemed to blame him for something he did not know had happened.

The chamberlain rose and stood before a door to Thomas' left. "The baron's son has suffered an accident, out riding earlier today," he said. "We've kept him here so as not to cause a disturbance, but our ability to treat him has been surpassed. He is in no small danger, and our need is becoming desperate enough that we thought, or that is, the baron thought, well–" The chamberlain braced himself as if about to do something unpleasant, opened the door, and gestured for Thomas to enter.

Inside Thomas saw a bed, and a boy some twelve years of age lay on his back atop the blankets. His eyes were closed, and a great bloody bandage was wrapped around his chest and over his left shoulder. "We thought we had the wound under control, but he was delirious for some time, and then unconscious," the chamberlain said. Thomas approached the bed, and saw that the boy was dead.

A hand grabbed Thomas' forearm from behind, and nails sank into his skin. "I am doing this as a kindness to the baron," the chamberlain's voice crawled into his ear. "He is fond of the boy, and has not taken his fall well. He is inconsolable, not in his right mind, and has begun to give strange orders. Were it me, I would sooner have you out in the snow, thrown back upon your vagrancy and your merited misfortunes, than to allow you to witness what's in this room. But as it is not me, it is his patience that privileges you to be here. I do what is ill-advised when my station demands it, but at the first whiff of skullduggery, I will put you in the ground." Thomas' arm was released, and the blood flowed to it again. A sob came from the room behind, and Thomas, who had still not taken his eyes off the dead boy, breathed deeply.

His mind went into motion, running through the contents of his satchel, and his path materialized before him, the bricks rising out of the abyss to meet his feet at each step. "It's a tricky thing," Thomas said, "and what you ask is not trivial. That is to say, there would first of all be the matter of the preservation of the boy's body – without it, he will... quite soon, you know." Thomas pictured the body of the boy stiffening, bloating, filling with maggots, and decaying.

"Just tell me whether you can do this thing. I must have your answer," the chamberlain said. "And I'll have no doublespeak."

"Something so subtle isn't a matter of just yes or no," Thomas said. "Truth be told, I could have no foreknowledge of my success, and even if it were done, it would take all of–" he paused, as if thinking "–a season–" he liked the liquid nature of that term, how it could be shaped and re-shaped to its container if need be "–to complete."

Thomas about-faced to meet the hostile eyes of the chamberlain and the captain of the guard. "Without me," he said, "the boy won't even have that chance, not by a long shot."

"I would require a proof of your abilities," the chamberlain said.

That was it, Thomas thought, his blood rising and flowing hard. "A token of what's to come, then," he said, and he reached gingerly into his satchel, fingering through it with a care to make no sudden movements. And there it was. I knew I would need it, he thought, and who can calculate the good it will now do me? God bless the brothers.

Thomas pulled the pale rod out of the satchel and held it before the chamberlain. The foot-long cylinder lay see-through in his grip, its transparency diluted by marbled streaks of gray and tiny white bubbles shot through its body, the latter like flecks of snow, as if the rod had trapped a portion of the winter within itself. Its surface bit at Thomas' palm, sapping and then numbing it with cold, but there was no mois-ture – a chunk of charmed ice, frozen into a permanent stillness. "If I may," Thomas said.

The chamberlain touched the rod with his fingertips, and recoiled, saying, "Let us see, then." The woman, Rebekah, was behind the other two men now, watching Thomas' hands intently. Thomas felt around the midsection of the rod with his thumb, seeking an unseen crease in it, and pressed; it snapped in half, sheer down the middle. Both pieces of the rod began to release a fine white mist from their cracked sides, and the air filled with a faint sweet smell and scarcely perceptible chill.

Thomas nodded to his onlookers, and with crazy blood, hoping as hard as his will would let him, he placed both segments on the floor, one to each side of the head of the bed; they stood upright like candles, the mist emanating from their tops. Stepping backward, he allowed that mist to escape and settle in the air, and it formed a sort of dome about the bed, just barely visible as the mist thinned, encompassing the boy and his surroundings.

"That's all," Thomas said. "If he remains there, he'll ward off the rot." The air was strange in that room now, subtly blessed, and Thomas entertained the thought that the force of this presence alone might win over his spectators. "I would have time to work," he told the chamberlain, after getting no immediate response. And then, to break the discomfort of another pause, "What would you have to lose?"

"It'll interfere with his right preparation, and burial," the guard said.

"You may have him removed at the first sign of the degradation of the body," Thomas said.

The chamberlain hesitated, then laid his hand upon the guard's shoulder. "I must speak to the baron. No one is to enter the paradise until I give the say-so," he said. "You," he went on to Thomas. "I want you out of here for now, to a place where you can play no tricks. And I want two days – if after two days your little gimcrack toy has proven its use, I will send for you to return."

And so that was how it was. The two days were given, and the two days passed: when the captain of the guard came for Thomas again, seated by the cornerstone of the church, Thomas' relief was total, and the possibilities flooded through him. The plans he had been fantasizing over gained a new solidity, and he wondered at the great result for so little effort.

Only the chamberlain awaited them in the cottage: Thomas looked for the baron, but still he was nowhere. The chamberlain sat at the table, his chin on his hands, a man who did not know how to show bafflement, much less gratitude, and so who approximated them with a faint annoyance. Thomas could see that the man's thoughts were already drifting away to matters in the distance, as though what was happening here had been settled. He said, "The baron has regained some of his vigor, and his faculties," and nodded towards the boy's room.

Thomas peeked within, and saw everything just as it was: the bed, the halves of the winter rod, the barely perceptible dome, and its barely perceptible chill and wholesome smell, not a trace of stink. And there in the middle of it all, the boy, as he was, utterly unchanged in death. Thomas turned back to the chamberlain, and saw that he had on the table a parchment, set beside a quill and inkwell. "Three months," the chamberlain said with a grave slowness, his knuckle rapping the parchment twice, once to accompany each word. "Your compensation to come only on your success."

Three months – an eternity.

"For your consideration," the chamberlain said, and handed Thomas the sheet of parchment.

Thomas moved his eyes over the ink on the paper from left to right at a comfortable but imperfectly steady pace, pressing forward in little leaps, sometimes retracing to the start of a line, or to the one just above it. When he reached the right edge of the symbols, he flicked his eyes across the page, to the left edge of the line below. He squinted slightly at several points, moving his lower eyelids up and his eyebrows down just enough to be visible, and he muttered almost inaudibly under his breath. When he reached the end of the ink, he grunted and said, "Very well, then," putting his hand forward to accept the quill that the chamberlain offered him.

The chamberlain pointed to a blank space beneath the end of the ink, on its right side. Thomas marked this exactly the way he had seen the old man do it – first with a little double swirl, and then with a series of nine glyphs, ordered from left to right. He held the quill tight, and focused his attention hard, praying for his dexterity not to fail him. But he had made this series of marks hundreds of times in practice, and he put each little line and curve in its order, and the symbols aligned straight with one another.

The chamberlain gave him a twitchy smile of office, and glancing at what he had written, said, "My thanks, then – brother Dioscorus." Dioscorus, Thomas thought – I'll remember.

III

The first day that Thomas set to work, it was insisted that he be observed by all three witnesses to the prior afternoon's events. The guard sat vigilant on a chair just inside the doorway of the boy's room, while the chamberlain was at the table by the entrance, occupied with his papers. Rebekah paced the cottage, frenetically in the morning and sulkily in the evening. After this first day's watch, so the chamberlain told him, only Rebekah would stay behind, to keep an eye on Thomas in perpetuity.

The boy's room had a low shelf jutting from the wall opposite the bed, and this made a workbench for Thomas to lay out his wizardly materials. From his satchel he produced an alembic, some vials of the old spikenard oil, and the box of explosive granules (the mustard aphrodisiac had all been sold), a deck-o'-many-things, a cairngorm peepstone, several painted wooden fetishes in the shape of Jasmine peasant spirits, a water-damaged medical grimoire, an ash-and-holly wand with one of Porphyry's teeth tied to the tip, a bundle of divining arrows, two ezroms of silver, a miniature weathervane, a homunculus garden, a handheld burning-glass, a pair of second-sight spectacles, a few black oak acorns, the begging bowl, a pouch of fairy dust, some trick knucklebones, a little pyramid of extraordinary density, a squirrel skull, some measures of magic mushrooms ground into powder, bottles of water and birch sap, a hunk of heliodor, a crucifix, a bundle of squincywort and another of valerian, a fishbone toothpick, a model of an Archimedes' screw, a divining cup with its tea leaves, and a parchment with the untranslated text of the Catalogue of Ships written on it.

Some contents of the satchel he kept within it, so as not to show his whole hand. What he did lay on the bench the guard watched with no small interest – some of the items he inquired about, and Thomas said something about them. With the collection arrayed, Thomas opened the medical book to a page with a diagram of the human body, which seemed the logical place to begin. "I just put everything out first," Thomas said, "as I often don't know beforehand precisely what will be needed" – the guard nodded.

It was simple enough to pass the time then. Thomas first looked over the boy closely, unwound his bandage, examined the wound and re-cleaned it, asked for a new bandage to replace the old, and set his focus on the grimoire, flipping the pages and scanning especially those with illustrations of the chest and shoulder. He felt for the boy's nonexistent pulse, snapped his fingers before his face, pinched his skin and tugged lightly at his hair, and held some liquid distilled by the alembic, and then some smelling salts, beneath the boy's nose. "Worth a try," he said to the captain, who seemed amused by the proceedings.

It was then time to begin in earnest: he asked for quill and parchment, and began scribbling various shapes, diagrams, symbols, and glyphs, many of which he was familiar with from the old man's writing. He rubbed his chin thoughtfully, made a few sketches, and then, evincing frustration, abandoned his visible train of thought and struck out what he'd put down. He snapped his fingers in realization and added ingredients to the homunculus garden; he dowsed the boy's body with the wand; he looked him over with the spectacles. When he needed to kill some time and think of what to do next, he mimed the motions of visiting the astral plane, which allowed him to sit cross-legged, eyes closed, without having to say or do anything for an hour or two – the procedure was familiar to anyone who'd seen a wizard, and no one would think to question it.

By the afternoon the captain, habitually overworked, was dozing; Rebekah said not a word all day. And at last the end of the day did come, and the two men, apparently satisfied, left Thomas shortly after sundown, calling Rebekah after them.

When they were gone, Thomas poked about the cottage. There was a little hall running across the back of the building past the entryway, cruddy with disuse and cluttered with junk. But then, wonder of wonders, a third room to the right of the entrance that housed another bed, double-sized. His amazement surpassed him: the granaries open to him, and a bed...some heavenly meddler was pulling strings, and he was in too much pleasure to be suspicious. The time he had yawned before him – imagine, he thought, to be left on the dole and forgotten, sleeping in this bed where no one could see me, forever. In the softness of this thought he could squint the vision of his mind and believe it were so.

And now, sleep, on a frame and beneath covers: fair Hypnos, reposing in a field of gray poppies. Each of the charities approaches him in turn as he breathes so softly that he might be mistaken for his brother, and each leans over, holding back her dark hair, to plant a kiss on his forehead. One kiss, two kiss, three, dropping from the dark hair above, from lips red like cherries, and they continue even once the charities have run out, cherries falling from above, off the great branches of a tree, plop, plop, each one on his forehead, to bounce off of him, roll, and lie still in the pile of cherries that blankets him.

The unmixed, doughy pleasure of that bed summoned the balm of that great god, who drew over him, endlessly seductive, forceful without effort. Thomas dimly remembered trifles like hunger, lust, and curiosity. They, like all the glitter of the universe, dissolved in his gentle omnipotence: when all treasures are tried, sleep is best.

Rebekah made good the next day on her duty to watch the boy. Her shufflings in the cabin woke Thomas early, though he could have slept for thirteen hours. He dressed, making sure the mantle was on before leaving the bedroom, and found her in the tiny hall, installing there a spinning wheel she had carried in. Thomas blinked at her as she skirted the bric-a-brac, scraping her shoes across the dust on the stone floor, and scooting the crates and chests about to clear a space. She dragged a folding stool and end table before the wheel, which she had set at the far end of the hall, and rose to sneeze and beat the cobwebs off her gown. She walked brusquely out of the hall and the cabin, locking eyes silently with Thomas as she left.

Thomas was sitting at the workbench in the boy's room, knocking his knuckles against the wood and wondering what to do about her, when she returned. She folded her arms and stood over him, too close, staring. Thomas pored over his materials, refusing to humor her, but soon relented and stared back. Still she said nothing, and continued to say nothing.

"Yes?" Thomas said.

"It's farcical," she said.

"Oh?"

"That you should be here. That I should be here, having to see–" she choked up slightly, pointing to the boy. "But that's just how it is, isn't it? Who fed and clothed him? Who nursed and changed him? Who taught him his left hand from his right hand? Me, I did all of it, so of course I would do this."

"You did, did you?" Thomas asked. "And where was his mother?" Her pause made clear it had been the wrong thing to say. Thomas lowered his eyes in shame.

"I can't even be left in peace to mourn," she said. "Without him, I don't know what I'm going to do. A complete waste, all of it, and now even the dignity of a decent death has to be taken away from us. Why couldn't you have died instead?"

"Well, give it a few years and I'll oblige," Thomas said. "For now, I can't control the whims of noblemen, or anything else."

"Don't speak about the baron. You don't know anything about him," Rebekah said. And then, "One day, one measly day – and now all of them have disappeared. They aren't here to watch their own lord's son. They aren't here to watch you, alone with him, doing God knows what," Rebekah said.

"The boy is dead. What more harm could I possibly do him?"

"How should I know? Maybe you'll pluck his brain out of his skull with tongs, pickle the pieces in a jar, and hawk them to a vagabond."

Thomas looked at her for a long time. "That's a good point," he said. "I guess I was wrong – it would be better if you stayed to keep watch, then."

This response was not the one she wanted, and she changed tracks. "You come making claims, but who will credit them? Blatherskites and children. I've seen nothing." She pointed to a candle standing in the corner where the workbench met the wall. "Light that," she said.

"I'm sorry?"

"Right now, light that candle."

Thomas looked politely puzzled. "It's daylight," he said.

"Even the most raggedy hedge wizard should be able to accomplish that much. That is the least – and the most – I would expect of you."

Thomas showed an innocent realization. "Oh, you mean me to ignite the wick magically. But I don't understand – haven't I already done greater things?"

"You won't do it. Yet what effort would it cost you?"

"It would cost me quite a lot of effort. If I lit that candle, you would ask me to do something else, or to do it again in the presence of other people, or accuse me of trickery. Since you're not well-disposed to me, you'll believe as you will."

"Isn't that tidy," Rebekah said. "You know all about what I would do, when it suits your convenience."

"I know it from experience – since in this very room you saw the power that preserves the boy, and yet you continue to insist."

"It was the rod that did that. Who knows how it works?"

"Oh, but you do know how the magical lighting of fires works?"

"These sophistries–" she spat the word "–may habitually work on any such rabble you're accustomed to bamboozle, but I don't know how yesterday you think I was born."

"Miss Rebekah," Thomas said, "I have no cause to think poorly of you in any way. Were I in your position, I would ask the same questions, and receive the same answers. When it's you who decide whether I come or go, you will undoubtedly do so."

And that was how the matter rested; they said nothing more to each other the rest of the day. Rebekah was now in the spinning room, now sitting by Thomas, just where the captain of the guard sat the day before. While she was there Thomas went through his motions, and she stayed vacant, it being beneath her to give him her interest.

As the sun started to set, Thomas left the cabin for the barony grounds, still saying nothing to Rebekah, and went to the mess hall by the guardhouse along the inner wall, where he was to be allowed a single meal each day. He ducked in and out quickly, ladling a bowl sheepishly, and eating outside to avoid conversing with any of the soldiers he knew. When he had finished, he stared at the empty bowl in his hands, and carrying it with him walked off to explore the grounds.

Thomas came upon a little courtyard in whose center grew a handsome cherry tree, its bare branches dusted with white and replete with mockingbirds. He entered by the western portal, and slipping into the arcade, found a bench facing the tree, and sat there to watch it.

His genius came to him as a painted bunting – a blue crown, red breast, and green wings, with the hues all bled together – and alighted on the cobbles. "Now that I'm a fool, I can wear splendid colors!" it chirped, and its cry was answered by the mockingbirds in the cherry tree. It kept its wings open, and flaunted them for the admiration of its audience, which tweeted a cacophony. It hopped in a circle, the setting sunlight hitting its wingspan from each angle, and Thomas saw all the colors in turn. When the red on its breast came around again to face him, the bird looked straight ahead for some moments, and its little black eyes shone smugly over its fat belly. It lowered its left wing, but held its right forward, and the crowd in the tree fell silent as the pinions pointed at him. "Thomas! Thomas! Thomas!" it cried.

"Here I am," Thomas said.

"Wizard! Aren't you afraid you'll be found out?"

"There's nothing to be found out," Thomas said. "Anyone who looks at me can see what I am."

"Wizard! Don't you care for anything at all?"

"That's unfair," Thomas said. "Everyone is dead."

"Wizard! And who will care for you?"

"No one," Thomas said. "But no one would have anyway. You've seen the fate of the boy."

With that the bunting lowered its other wing, and the mockingbirds sang again, together in monophony. It was the actor's lament, and Thomas enjoyed it. But there was a woman passing through the courtyard, who marveled at the birds singing in unison – and when they noticed, they fell off, and the genius and its bright colors were gone. Thinking enough time had passed, Thomas picked himself up to return to the mess, and ate again.

IV

There was a ritual that Thomas and Rebekah enacted. Thomas left the room with the bed each morning to find Rebekah already arrived; she said to him, "Good morning, Dioscorus," and he said to her, "Good morning, Rebekah," and that sealed them against any obligation to speak to one another, until the powers of the spell were to be renewed the next day.

The boy's room had begun to fill with objects, hers and his. She'd placed votive candles on the floor, by the cracked frost cylinders near the head of the bed, to be lit each evening after she opened the window. Thomas didn't care for the cold this let in, but thought it best not to gainsay her. There were her hand-weaving materials, too, heaped up on the floor to the side of the door, and spilling off the end table she had put there, to work where she could watch the boy. And then there were her scrolls, which her literacy and access of unclear provenance to the barony's archives permitted her. They had been strewn about, furled and unfurled, their dark characters mocking him. Thomas' workbench slipped into increasing disaster, a fine portrait of the mad wizard at work – he made scores of half-baked things, on the time and materials of the barony.

Rebekah had begun to speak to the boy, calling him by name. There was more to talk about with a dead person than a living one, and she spoke unabashedly in the presence of Thomas – never to him, always to the boy. She would ask the boy what he had done that day, and give him news of his father; she would opine about the people they knew, and why they were deserving of damnation; she would read to him aloud from the scrolls by the light of the fireplace in the opposite wall, before leaving for the night.

Thomas perceived things only in their contrasts, and did not bother with detail if it did not bother him – it was up to his surroundings to make their presence known, by being loud enough to force his attention. For this reason it became difficult to tell the days apart, because all of these things were always there: the cottage, the paradise, the workbench, the mess of accoutrements, the winter, the boy, Rebekah. The spell in the morning, the day spent with her talking past him to a corpse, the fire in the evening and then the bed frame again. It didn't matter whether this were bizarre: he had lost the sensitivity for such things, and in any case everything was just as bizarre as everything else at the end of it, so he had become subdued, and his troubles theoretical.

It was Rebekah's continued attention to the boy that made Thomas notice his peculiarities, a boy that he would never have given another thought to, as he lay there in permanent state. Hair and fingernails that did not grow, and, he supposed, a body that did not grow either – the dome encased him as if in clear quartz, a model from which the author of the medical grimoire might have drawn his diagrams. His wound, too, lay in state: never healing and never worsening, its bandage was replaced until the blood ceased to seep from it, though it never closed. And it was then, when the boy had become entirely stable, that the question of what to do with his body in the meantime came to press upon Rebekah.

That body was done with sweat, snot, vomit, urine, feces – but still it accumulated more ordinary filth, the sort that comes not from being alive, but from merely being in the world. And so Rebekah took him from the bed every several days to bathe him, relocating him to a wash-tub in the main room of the cottage to scrub his nude body. This was the reason that Eudoxia, Rebekah's sister-in-law from a saner and more es-tablished branch of the family, began appearing in the cabin: a second pair of arms was needed to carry out the ablutions. As best Thomas un-derstood, Eudoxia was not supposed to be there, but there appeared to be no one to stop her, so that she became a more regular presence in the cottage with the passage of time, keeping company with Rebekah in her sewing room, and laughing a bit too often.

Eudoxia was a woman of several temperaments, none of them agree-able to Thomas; she eyed him often, like a disapproving chaperone. She was the sort of person who should have had an asymmetrical face, and Thomas was amused to find himself thinking, out loud in his head, "You aren't supposed to be here," as if that mattered to him, and as if he were not just expressing his own native distaste for this woman, who created a contrast and interrupted the haze he had settled into. He allowed him-self that much introspection, but took it all in stride, knowing that it was fine for certain people to be made to dislike each other, and finding his dislike no more troublesome to him than any of the other sentiments it was his lot to live with.

The two women began to dress the boy, plainly at first, but then in fine outfits: his clean hair shone over glittering doublets as he lay on the bed. And so whenever he was bathed, the wake began anew, and Thomas was forced to see him anew, and his somber stillness became ever so slightly less pleasant.

One afternoon, Rebekah said to the boy, "And there's never a moment to oneself in the fort. You know how it is, there's always someone around." And so Thomas broke his silence toward her, and made a point of telling her that he had to procure something from the apothecary, and that he would be gone for some time, hoping that this would be enough to satisfy her. It was a passable enough excuse, as he went to the apothecary fairly regularly, to gather materials on the baron's permit that he might use in the mixing of drugs. Each time he bought something, the apothecary told Thomas, "Brother Dioscorus, I'm praying for the recovery of the baron's son," and Thomas replied, "Good lady, I endeavor to answer those prayers."

Thomas did not go to the apothecary, but ate in the mess, and then wandered the grounds of the barony within the inner wall, moving slowly so as to delay his return, and ruminating over the items he had thus far collected in the cottage – how much each might be worth, and at what time near the end of the three months it might be best to leave with them, and flee the Hellebore.

In his distraction Thomas drifted too close to the guardhouse, and heard, "There's the man!" He turned himself around to see Oliver and Wyatt at the range: they were drinking and throwing axes at a scarecrow. Oliver grinned at Thomas, steadying the haft in his grip and wobbling slightly on his feet, and he threw just as he turned his attention back to the target. His aim was deteriorating: the toss flew way wide of the torso, and the back of the axehead smashed into a bunch of empty mugs and bowls that had been left on the lid of a barrel, and fell to the dirt. "Hey,

Tom," he said drawling, "I've got a kid sick back home. Why don't you fix her up for me?" Oliver picked up his stein from the ground by his feet, and laughing staggered to go fetch his weapon.

Wyatt wasn't as deep in the drink as his comrade, and bade Thomas to throw with them.

"You'll ruin the blades," Thomas said.

"They're already ruined. Here, come on." Wyatt pressed his axe to Thomas' hand, but it stayed limp, and refused to move to take it.

"No, no!" Oliver yelled from his position by the scarecrow. "If he's going to have a go, you'd better make him stand farther back. It's too easy sober from that distance," he said, motioning to a line they had drawn in the dirt. "Look, you can both throw at once!" he yelled. "Let me just–" and he swept the remaining mugs and plates off the barrel he had hit, letting them clatter to the ground. He wrapped himself around the barrel, and hugging it tight, began twisting left and right as he stepped backward, dragging the barrel along the ground with him. Oliver panted hard and laughed between twists, scooting closer to his goal inch by inch as Wyatt and Thomas looked on.

A dog was watching them, as far beyond the threat of their throws as it could get while still being party to the game – a doleful little brown thing, the sort with eyes that were always looking upward, so that the whites were large beneath the irises. It stood up with its head dipped low, preemptively cringing, and now looked at Thomas pleadingly.

Wyatt's gaze became abstracted. "I don't know why we're still in the Hellebore," he said. "The work is about to run out, I know it. It's been quiet here for so long – children are playing outside the walls unattended. Once the winter ends, I don't know what's going to happen to us."

Thomas turned and saw Wyatt in profile. "Go home, Wyatt," he said.

"Come spring there might be work further west, they say, around the Sterseymouth," Wyatt said, still not turning to look Thomas in the eyes. "You should come with us, Tom. If you're going to earn your keep being a flunky, you may as well crack some heads – drive Jordan's men into the sea. I bet we could stay on for a full year."

That suggestion warmed Thomas, but he knew it to be unserious. "There won't be enough fighting to fill a year," he said, "not even on the coast. Wyatt, you should go home."

Oliver had finished positioning the second barrel to the right of the first, and was mounting a second scarecrow on top of it, sticking its pole of a spine through a hole in the lid. Wyatt tried to put the axe in Thomas' hand again: he grabbed his wrist, and placed the haft against it, ingenuously confounded by the geometry of the two objects, and their refusal to stick together. Wyatt moaned, gripped the axe himself, and stepped to the throwing line. Thomas gasped and moved to stop him, but he was too slow, and the axe flew. It whizzed just past Oliver, who was still standing next to the barrel, and lodged itself right in the brow of the newly erected scarecrow, tearing the straw head off its shoulders. The watching dog flinched, and walked in a wide arc that angled away from Oliver and then back toward Thomas.

"Hey, hey, that's the way!" Oliver roared, removing the axe from the scarecrow's soft skull, and holding both weapons triumphantly above his head, one in each hand. He tossed them both back to the dirt, and jovially began mounting the head of the fallen scarecrow on its pole afresh. "Up you go again, my man," he said.

The dog had reached Thomas, and was licking the back of his hand. Thomas moved to scratch behind its ears and then to rub its neck, and at this it shifted to licking the inside of his wrist. When he stopped petting it, it bobbed its nose against his fingers, tossing them lightly upward. As he turned to leave, ignoring Oliver's protests, the dog followed him some ways. Thomas recalled the crust he had stuffed in his satchel on leaving the mess, and tossed it to the ground. The dog was now occupied, and Thomas was able to make his way back to the wooded enclosure.

Thomas reentered the cottage to find that he had not spent enough time away. He caught Rebekah at her devotions, leaning over the boy in silence.

It struck Thomas as indulgent, this long grief, wallowing in the delusion that there was a special torment in the death of some one boy over all the others, and this at a time when the arrows of fortune had been dulled from overuse. How many variations on this scene could be played out, before the old threat – "I'll give you something to really cry about" – rang hollow, because there was nothing left, in the quiver or the eyes, to make good on it? But then her lament worked some alchemy. It wasn't her keenness of feeling which moved him, but her manner: she had a weird way of weeping, hunched over the body, eyes squinched to keep the tears behind the sluice gates, and lots of small spasms in the shoulders. He had never seen anyone mourn in this way before, and as her sufferings and his were incommensurate, the pains were made new. He stood behind her and placed his hand on her shoulder.

Rebekah did not stop, supposing, it seemed, that it would now be purposeless to do so.

V

Once Thomas had seen her mourning, Rebekah did not keep up the rigor of her watch at the cottage. She was sometimes not there when Thomas awoke. Some days she left before sunset for her dinner, and did not return; and there came a few days during which Thomas did not see her at all, and was left to his own resources, being finally granted his keen solitude. There is no being alone like being left alone, which is not like having been alone all along: when the outlines of the departed still linger, and leave an impression of their absence, that contrast is the only thing that can reveal the state's subtle, savory core. Well, in truth, Thomas was not alone – the boy was there. On the first day that Rebekah failed to appear, Thomas looked to him, still on display with his long, still eyelashes, and said, "Isn't that funny? I'm the only one left."

But in truth, Rebekah had not gone – her habits had only rearranged, as the nature of her situation became clear to her, and her life slid slowly back to its normal rhythms. She returned, and still washed and dressed the boy with Eudoxia, though not so often as before, and she spoke to him less, and more poignantly, as one speaks to a departed relative in prayers, rather than to a member of the household. The goal of Rebekah's speech was getting murkier, and placed as it was between greater gulfs of silence, it was often a mystery whether it was meant for the boy, or Thomas, or herself, or no one, or God. Thomas felt the intimacy of her soliloquizing to be inappropriate, but always attended to it curiously.

There is more to a person's presence than what is said or done. Rebekah's hanging around was making it increasingly difficult to concentrate, so that Thomas was in two minds as he began to dread being perceived by her, and the boy was fading in proportion as she appeared, so that it was as if a doll were in the room between them, a human shape always at the edge of consciousness. As the clutter grew worse, Rebekah would pile her materials on the bed next to him, so that he lay surrounded by combs and distaffs. Her time in the room became erratic – she was gone for long enough that he became accustomed to her absence, but then she would appear again without warning, and without salutation, and sit there for what seemed like forever. He would carve his trinkets slowly, and too deliberately, so that his hands felt unsure, and the thought of looking away from the bench, or even away from his hands, pained him.

She had also begun to eat in the cottage, bringing Eudoxia with her from the grounds during the midday. They would set a place for him, and he took it up – the three of them spoke to each other curtly as they ate, and the women's demeanor became easy again when they retreated to the spinning room. And then one day Thomas' fears were realized, and he was left alone with Eudoxia at that table, as Rebekah left the cottage to fetch something mid-meal.

Eudoxia was mischievous with delight, as if she had been waiting for the right moment to truly speak to him. The tresses of her hair were suddenly visible to him, and seemed accusatory in how tightly they were wound; he wanted to cut them off. "Well, Tommyrot," she said, "How are we doing?"

"Hmm," Thomas said. He looked into her eyes stolidly, and refused to look away before she did.

"You know," she said, "the final day of the month is one of great magical power. Do you plan to make use of it?"

"Make use of it?" Thomas said. "What are you talking about?"

"Well, I thought a wizard like you would know," Eudoxia said. "That's when the stars align, and great things are possible. A spell cast on that day is worth a thousand cast on any other day of the year. Surely that would be when you made your move?" A smirk tugged at the corners of her lips.

Thomas recalled the revival of the boy, and exhaled.

"Don't tell me you don't believe in the influence of the heavenly bodies on earthly affairs?" she asked. "Everything on the earth has its duplicate in the heavens. An alignment here corresponds to an alignment there. But you know all of this, of course!"

"The stars do undoubtedly have some influence on what happens beneath them," Thomas said, "but probably none that anybody should care about. I would be more worried about how things are aligned in the Hellebore, if I were you."

"Well, what do *you* know!" Eudoxia said. "The world is full of surprises, Tommyrot. I can't imagine who could doubt your wisdom, or your inevitable success. I can see the baron's hopes fulfilled now – and Rebekah's."

"You're a pleasant interlocutor, and your concern for the ones you love is touching," Thomas said. And they remained quiet until Rebekah returned.

Rebekah had picked up another new habit: while her reading to the boy had become more sporadic, the time that she spent on it during any one day lengthened and lengthened, until her storytelling sessions became events in their own right. She would set herself up in the corner of the room, by the boy's head, with the chair positioned just next to the frost cylinder and the votive candle, and read what she claimed to be his favorite portions of scripture. How could the boy have so many favorites, Thomas wondered – how were there even enough of these scriptures to exhaust so much time, without their ever being finished?

Some of these stories he had heard before, more or less as she read them; others were the same only in outline as what he had been told, and others were bizarre to him, telling of people that were nothing like him, and whose exploits had nothing to do with the world he inhabited, and whose moods he had no way of understanding. It struck him still as odd that she knew how to read all of these things, and was given the scrolls so freely. He suspected that anyone who could read would be in danger of contact with such stuff, and would come away from it with an unwholesome mind.

When she sat there in the corner, Thomas never turned to face her, but kept himself strictly toward the bench. He knew that her eyes were some-times on him; his neck would grow ever so slightly warmer, and he heard her breathe in and out, carrying the faintest contour of her voice, during those pauses when the parchment rustled and she regained her place. In and out, the rhythms went on, halted, and went on again: kings and saints in the gloom, all given life by her vowels and drenched in myrrh, moved about and made to vanish like breath. And when she had been speaking for some time, it seemed that the sound seeped into the walls, and made them cushions instead of timber and daub, and the feeling in his neck crept up and spread out over the dome of his skull, bathing it in a soporific tingle.

Things were changed – and changed again, when it was night, and in the chill of the dying embers he turned at last to ponder the vacant chair where she had been.

One evening the story ended as she sat there – the narration of the wars of the Lord broke off, and Rebekah was silent for a while. "Well, I'd best get going," she said. "I suppose you're tired of listening to me anyway." That suggestion was a delicately prepared thing, he saw, a veil spun from such fine gossamer that it could be broken through without resistance, and whose semi-transparent artifice concealed the layers of labor behind it. But he had nothing to give back in kind, and so he responded in the only way his nature would allow him.

"Nonsense," he said. "I very much enjoy your reading. It's kind of you to keep us company." He turned back to her, and she had no visible reaction to that answer, but just looked again at the parchment, and read on a while longer before getting up to go.

There's no good way to describe what happened to how Thomas and Rebekah treated each other after that. The inward shift is best inferred from its external signs: she began to accompany him on his errands, and he accompanied her on hers, seeing the insides of several of the manors on the grounds; they became a regular fixture at Mass in the chapel, sitting next to one another in the pew; and when the mood struck them, they slept together in the cottage.

Thomas had never considered before whether he were attractive, and so he asked Rebekah if he was, and she told him that he wasn't. He asked her whether she wanted to know if she were attractive – she told him that he wouldn't be a relevant judge of such a thing anyway, so it didn't much matter either way what he said. But in any case Thomas did give his opinion, and said that she was neither attractive nor unattractive, though she was extraordinarily pleasant, which he thought was a far better thing. They moved very slowly around each other, and spoke less to each other again as the days passed, but now the silences were easy.

Thomas had begun, in spite of himself, to think of the boy by name now; it was because she had used the name so often, and he had listened too closely to what she said. Not too long more, he thought: my skull is starting to freeze. He wondered dully whether she might offer a path to staying in the baron's employ – the boy, after all, did not have to live, and did not really have to die, as no one really needed to do either of these things. But this made him shiver, and he was not pleased with having entertained the thought as long as he did, the cold seeming to him suddenly an insufficient excuse for it.

On the final day of January, Thomas exited the paradise, whose trees obscured the night sky, and from the courtyard of the cherry tree, next to a plot that in spring would have tulips in it, looked at the stars. No, in fact, they did not seem to him any more potent than they usually were that night. He found the Bull and the Hunter, but they seemed to him spindly things, hanging fragile from the firmament, and their shapes were uncertain. He drew their outlines with small variations, as it suited his imagination, and severed their limbs and grafted new ones onto them; he fused them together into frightening amalgams, and drew them apart again. He drew entirely new beasts, letting his eyes wander over patterns he had never put together before – and they amused his mind until he saw that the new shapes were no less spindly than the old. The Hunter may be watching, he thought, but so what then? And he returned to his cottage, to put a roof between him and the stars.

VI

Thomas became torpid as the weeks wore on. As no one was watching him, he began to spend more time lazing in the wood near the quarters, sitting and smoking against the cottage wall and catching snowflakes on his tongue, or walking back and forth along the inner side of the lesser wall of the paradise. It struck him one day that, as wonderful as it always was to be momentarily forgotten by authority, his complacency might get him killed – and anyhow his smoke was nearly gone. And so with a view to seeing some of his fellow men again, he set out back to the grounds of the barony, and then past the gate back out into town. But he understood as he was among the buildings that what he really wanted to see was the open world, and so he made his way to the green beyond the palisade.

The snow was slight on the even ground after a brief thaw, and a bright, dry cold suffused the air – the sort that ices the blood just mildly, and picks at the skin without bothering it. A mob of children were playing at war there in the open. They ran and leapt after each other, and the movements were only partly sensical, following as they did the fancies of their makers, so that attackers became retreaters, and spears became bows or siege engines, and there was much dispute as to who was on what side, and as to who was or wasn't dead.

Thomas went past them and sat at the foot of the threshing floor wall to watch. They stabbed each other, mimed the spray of blood and the spilling of entrails, formed and broke ranks, toppled bodies to the ground and hauled them by the feet to arrange them in rows. They commanded one another, with puffed chests and pointed fingers, and shouts that carried across the frosted green; they wrestled on the ground, choking their opponents and beating them with their fists. Thomas watched them all, and his eyes twitched.

Within a few minutes Mary, who was among them, spotted Thomas seated at the wall again, and dragging along her brother Peter, who was just shy of her in age, broke from the tumult and raced over to meet him.

"Mr. Wizard! Where have you been? How come we haven't seen you?" she asked breathlessly.

"Oh, I've had some business past the inner wall," Thomas said.

"I heard the baron's son is sick."

"That's so."

"I hope he gets better – everyone says the baron would go mad if something happened to him."

"You have no reason to worry. He'll be fine."

"We're doing the king's war," Peter said, with the conviction of the young that whatever is happening needs explaining.

"Did you fight the king, wizard?" Mary asked.

Thomas considered her for a moment, wondering at the spite in her eyes – an innocent spite, for which conquest and play weren't distinguished. "Wizards don't fight in wars, Mary," he said gently.

"Well, they should!" she snapped. "My dad says so, too. He says they're cowards."

"If the wizards fought the king," Peter said, "they'd have killed him right away."

"If I were a wizard," Mary went on, "I would have turned all the soldiers into cockroaches. Then I would have lit the king on fire. They would've been sorry they ever even tried." She reared up her arms and rose to her tiptoes, swelling her cheeks with air, and mimed the stoking of a great flame with her hands, exhaling through her teeth to mimic its roar. She lowered herself as her breath ran out, dwindling until she couldn't press her lungs anymore, and coughing lightly as she gave up. "And then, when he was just a pile of ash, I would blow him away." And she puffed out her cheeks again, and blew across the ground. "Goodbye, forever, Your Majesty."

Peter laughed. "You'd probably screw it up, or his guards would find you and take you in," he said. Assuming the pose of a soldier, with his left arm clutching an invisible shield before his breast, and his right fist closed about an unseen weapon, he bellowed, "What's all this, then? The king is dead, and that magic man has burned him up? I'll kill you, rebel!"

"A soldier couldn't kill a wizard!" Mary said.

"Oh, yes he could! Dad told me what the king's soldiers would do – they could kill anyone. They wouldn't care if you were a wizard or not." Peter hacked forward at the air several times, giving each stroke a little onomatopoeia. "And here, look," he said, grabbing Thomas by the hand and pulling him up from his seat. "They don't take prisoners – if they caught you, this is how they'd execute you." He reached to the back of Thomas' right leg and slashed across it, hamstringing him.

Thomas cried out and fell to his knees, moaning as the blood gushed out of him. He was forced forward to steady himself on his palms, exposing his neck and shoulders. "And then–" Peter said, rearing back, and holding the weapon high. He stabbed downward and planted the blade into the soft skin between the neck and collarbone. "This is what we do to traitors!" he shouted, holding the blade in place, deep in the flesh, twisting it, and then rearing his arm back in triumph, to release the weapon and let the blood flow again. Thomas saw crimson over the grass, heard the sounds of battle, and blackness clouded his eyes: he fell forward in a heap, and lay crumpled on the ground. There was a small voice at the back of his mind: "Thomas! Thomas! Thomas!" His muscles didn't so much as twitch, and his midsection was still, without the rise and fall of his breath.

"Oh my God, Peter!" Mary cried. "What did you do? I think you really killed him!"

"No way!" Peter said, though his voice quavered. The two of them crouched over Thomas' body, and then knelt beside him. "Hey," Peter said. "Wake up." He placed his hands on Thomas' back, and shook him lightly, but there was no response. "Hello?" He turned Thomas' head to face him, and lifted one of his eyelids, but there was no resistance or acknowledgment. "Hello? Mr. Wizard?" He released Thomas' head, letting it thump hard to the grass.

"Oh no, Peter, you idiot!" Mary said. "We have to go get help!"

That got Thomas going again. His eyes were open, and he jolted upright. "Aha!" he cried, causing Mary and Peter to flinch backward and squeal with delight.

"I knew it!" Mary said. "I knew you were just playing dead! A wizard can't die."

"You did not!" Peter said. "I saw how scared you were. He really had you going. You really thought a pretend sword could kill him! How could it do that, it's not even real!"

"Shut up!" Mary shouted, and pushed her brother from the side, causing him to reel and stumble away as he laughed. "I don't know how magic works."

"Oh, I'm alive alright," Thomas said. He lowered the pitch of his voice, and rubbed the folds of his throat together to make it demonic. "And I'm furious!" he shouted, springing to his feet, bearing his teeth like fangs, and holding his hands open before him like claws. "You'd better run, little children!"

Mary and Peter scrambled over themselves to run off, giggling madly. It was uncanny, Thomas thought, how fast they were – how quickly and utterly they could get themselves away from something that was no threat to them. He watched them as they scampered toward the palisade, not stopping to look back, giggling and panting all the while, until he could hear them no more, and they disappeared into the town. Thomas saw that the remaining soldiers on the green had finished their business, and the victors were now in a ring dividing spoils. He looked again to where he had seen Mary and Peter last at the gate, and had a desire to see Rebekah.

The two of them lay together that evening in the quarters' bed, as the afterglow faded. Thomas was playing with Rebekah's right hand. With his index finger he traced its outline, drawing the curve of each finger to its apex, then sliding down the valleys to the gaps in between: slow and fast by turns, changing direction on a whim, pressing and alleviating the pressure, picking lightly at the webbing. He peered at her hand closely as its palm faced him, to catch all of the infinitesimal movements of the digits and twitches of the joints. Her head was on his shoulder, and she watched her own hand as he did, though not intently, her attention occupied by her speech.

"When he was alive," Rebekah said, "he would ask me about all sorts of things – miscellanies, you know. He wanted to know what certain birds were named, or he wanted to know why it was harder to walk uphill than downhill. Of course you have to know when to bother to answer a child's questions. But now I think – why was I the one expected to tell him those things? And what does it really matter, if anything he might have learned has disappeared now? I read a lot – and there is a lot of useless trivia."

Thomas squeezed the pad at the tip of Rebekah's index finger, pressing his thumb into it, then moved down below the knuckle, to squeeze the midsection – and he went on doing this for each segment of each of her fingers, as if documenting the tension in each of them. He placed his hand beneath hers, and laced his fingers through hers from behind, and curled, so that Rebekah's hand curled with his. She offered no resistance, but made no response, and holding her like that Thomas reached his thumb around to her palm, and traced the outline of the triangle where the wrinkles met at its center.

"I wonder, sometimes," Rebekah said. "I've wondered it before, but now having to see the boy every day, there and yet not gone, I think about it more and more often. If our death is where our true life begins, I don't know why we're meant to avoid it. There are reasons given – but I always forget what they are. I can't remember, because the question is real to me, but the answers aren't, and they run out of my head like water out of a sieve. If I really thought the boy were in paradise, what would I have to grieve? And yet I do – the grief is real, but what I tell myself to keep it at bay is unreal."

"Rebekah," Thomas said, and released her hand. "Whatever it is Eudoxia might say about me–" He was embarrassed at not knowing how to continue, and left the thread for her to pick up. Rebekah propped herself up on her elbow, and looked at him without malice or illusion.

"And what, pray tell, would Eudoxia have to say about you?" It would be an insult, it seemed, to imply that there could ever be anything, about Thomas or any other matter, that Eudoxia could discover but that she could not. She held his gaze for a few moments, then thew herself down again, her arms to her sides, looking to the ceiling.

"Rebekah," he said. "You know that I may not be able to do it."

She lay unmoving, and her eyes drifted shut. "That makes you no worse than any other man," she said. And Thomas lay awake for a long while.

VII

Two days on, Thomas asked in town after the witch in the woods, and the Meikeljohns claimed to have seen her. He took their hazel rod in both hands as he was instructed, and made his way into the trees, taking the turns it divined for him: the cottage wasn't there, and had to be come at roundabout-ways. So he went left and then right, and around in a spiral, following the climbers on the boles until things got deeper and darker in the midday, on through the which-way in the wych wood. With the rowan berries in his satchel he braved the claws of the balding elms, and the odd badger fled before him, leaving its prints in the thin snow – all to find the Christmas roses, which were where the witch was. He saw them at last, in a bunch before a stump with an irregular hollow through its massive side. And though he could see clear to the other end and the cold woods beyond, when he crawled through he emerged in a clearing, kept in preternatural green against the winter.

There was a young woman there, lying on her back in the grass within a ring of toadstools, with a leg across her knee, and squinting up against the sunshine at the bell of a foxglove she held between her fingers.

Thomas came to her, careful not to tramp on the flowers, and as he stood over her he saw that her hands were stained at the fingertips, with an ambiguous cool hue – not a dyer's hands, but a forager's, and maybe a brewster's. He opened his own palm for her, so she could see the green streaks across it, pale but unmistakable.

"I suppose you'll be wanting to see the hag, then," she said resignedly, still squinting.

"You're not her?" Thomas asked.

"Don't even," she said, getting to her feet and tossing the foxglove aside. "Over there."

The cottage sat at the edge of the clearing, formed out of and fused into the gargantuan oaks that bounded the wood. The trees had too many branches, and they gnarled about each other in too many directions – splayed out as if their dryads were caught mid-step in a mean conjuring dance, their rituals hardened into stillness by the witch's guile. The steepled fingers of several oaks met and crossed to form the rafters, on which lay a mess of thatch, and the cottage's back half was cut out of one of the massive trunks. The arrangement was meant to affect the perceiver at night – the daylight made the display incongruous, as if the trees were overeager, unsettling only in an unintended way.

Thomas followed the apprentice as she approached the cottage's front, this a wall of sheer wood without visible joint or cut. There was no entry, and so she made one, sticking her fingers into the wood to make the outline of a doorframe appear, and flinging the face of the cabin open, as if the portion of the wall within this outline were on a hinge. Without looking at Thomas, she entered, and sat herself on a large chest to the right of the opening, saying nothing, her work finished.

The air clotted with the smell of earth and rot, covered over with cloying lilac. Crows scattered as Thomas entered, swarming and cawing about the rafters, and disturbing the thyme, entrails, and rabbit corpses that hung there. Thomas held his vomit in and let his eyes adjust to the dimness, and saw the witch catty-corner from the apprentice, across the room with her back turned to both of them, pecking at something on the dirt floor. She ruffled her feathers, cast her head around to eye Thomas, and pulled the cloak of the crow-form off of herself, to appear before him as a woman clothed in a mess of black shawls and feathers. She approached him with an air split down the middle between mischief and scorn, and finishing her appraisal of him in moments, she spoke to the apprentice.

"I ought to be harder on you, Miranda," she said, "for continuing to attract refuse. The colors offend me, and the face on this one does no one any favors either – you ought at least, if you can't stop being a bird-lime for these types, to have better taste." Miranda made no particular response to the witch, but swung her foot out and back rhythmically, allowing her heel to kick the chest on which she sat, so that its metal latch clinked with the force of each thump. The witch snapped at Thomas: "Well, what do you want out of me?"

"I need to raise someone," Thomas said. "A boy who's died on me."

"Have you got a corpse? You can't mean to assemble him after all his bits have been scattered. Even for the creator on judgment day, that's an impressive trick. Well, He says He can do it, anyway, but we haven't seen that yet."

"No, I have the body alright," Thomas said.

"And how fresh is it?"

"How fresh does it need to be?"

"If you're talking seriously about the reanimation of dead flesh," the witch said, "then your time is limited. Let it rot for even a few days, and what you'll have is a pus bag, not a person – there will be no organs left to work the body, even if you manage to get it moving." She poked Thomas in the stomach to illustrate.

"I've had the boy's body for two months," Thomas said. "But I held it on the day of death in a freeze, using a damping wand of some sort."

The witch goggled at him, and at last smiled. "You just sit tight right there," she said. "An intact body? I have just the thing. Yes, I'll make the boy stand upright, just as nice as if coming out of a nightmare, and no more than that. Animating tonic, yes–" she fumbled her hand over the wrinkles on her brow, and muttered, "What with oyster meat and quick-lime, aha. Allow me a moment and I'll fetch you it."

And then she was gone, behind a low curtain that led somewhere in the back of the cottage. Miranda remained impassive, still kicking the chest backwards, and looked at Thomas as if to tell him that he was very bad at knowing what to ask for. After a few moments of staring at each other, he nodded to her. "Miss."

"Are wizards so desperate these days, or I suppose just incompetent?" she asked.

"I wouldn't know," Thomas said.

"Anyhow, my advice would be to let it go," she said. "Whoever it is that died, I mean."

"I will take your advice into consideration," he said. The two of them waited in silence for several minutes, Miranda diligently scratching the front of her teeth with a fingernail. They listened to the witch cursing under her breath as she moved jars and opened cabinets behind the curtain.

When the hag emerged, she held a corked vial filled with an orange liquid. "Here it is!" she said, wiggling it back and forth so that the mixture sloshed against the glass.

"Here is what? What is it – exactly?" Thomas asked.

"Well, aren't you a bright one!" the witch said. "Well, it's what you asked me for, isn't it? This will wake up your boy."

"If you don't mind my suspicion," Thomas said, "I'd like some proof of that, or how about a demonstration, if you like – to know that what is in there is what you claim."

"Well, Miranda, our buddy wants to know if my potions work!" The witch let her eyes grow wide. "Yet I can't blame someone for not being a dupe. Let's go, then." And she swept out of the doorway that Miranda had pulled out of the wood.

Thomas followed her, with Miranda lagging a bit behind him in stolid curiosity, as the witched guided him into the oaks. She led him on for some time, a rustle of black feathers, in the crow-form and out of it, making so many turns that after some time Thomas lost his way – and her speed was unrelenting, so that he had to catch her continuously out of the corner of his eye, and listen to her movements as she flitted through the branches above and ungracefully ruffled the ground below. At last Thomas hopped over a fallen log, to find that the witch had stopped in the middle of a ring of trees. He approached her, with the apprentice at his side as if she were glued to him, to see that the witch held a dead rat, clutching its tail in a fist, so that its body dangled in the air.

She uncorked her vial, laid the rat across her palm, and meticulously allowed a single drop of liquid to fall onto the corpse. The rat awoke: or its eyes were opened, and its spine went erect, and all its digits taut. It jerked itself upright, and raised itself on its hind legs, and let its front paws hang limp before its chest, the pose of a begging dog. It fawned at the witch, its nose twitching with its head at strict attention, and the slightest murmur came from it, as it nervously awaited instruction.

The witch held her other bony hand above the rat, and pulled at it as if with invisible strings – she raised and lowered her fingers, and in time with them the rat raised and lowered its joints. She made it bow to Thomas, and then perform a crude jig. With each motion, a hissing emerged from the rat, like a suppressed scream, and its body shuddered as its nose quivered.

"That creature is unwell," Thomas said. "It seems to be in pain."

"Pain!" the witch cried. "Well, look here, Miranda! Bringing the *dead* back to *life* –" she bulged her eyes in time with the emphasis of her words – "It appears as though that weren't a *cozy* enough business for our *wizard* here. Well hey, we've all felt a little *pain* before, have we not, Miranda, and what's the worst it's done for us?"

Miranda turned her gaze from the rat to the witch, and then to Thomas, and shrugged. The witch went on, "Perhaps up in the clouds where you live, *wizard*, there is no *pain*, and so having *lived* without it you'd expect to *die* without it, and live *again*, hey? I'll tell you about pain, you daft little shaver. I've had four children, two lived, and that was *pain* – you probably don't even know you were wrenched out of your mother's body, and so caused her *pain* just by coming into existence, all so you could stand there with that stupid look on your face. My daughter starved to death in the winter famine up at the Hyacinth, and I'm sure that was *pain*ful. *Pain* is what makes everything happen, and you wizards get squeamish when you see it."

Each time the witch stressed one of her words, she allowed her knuckle joints to twitch, and the unseen strings puppeteering the rat shifted, causing its limbs to spasm as it shrieked, then returned to its stance groveling. "Ask the creator how He feels about *pain*," the witch said. "Over half of creation, the animals not excluded, I'm sure, are sent into the unquenchable fires, eternal and unsleeping, unblinking, to exist for no other reason than to be in *pain*. I have probably rescued this rat from just such a fate, so that it might have some moments' reprieve, and it obeys me from sheer gratitude."

"If you would not do that," Thomas said.

"Alright," the witch said, and she relaxed her hand, leaving the rat limp again. She looked about her, and seeing the knothole in the trunk of the oak by her side, tossed the rodent's corpse into it. "Is that a no, then, on the animating tonic?"

"A no, yes, I'm afraid," Thomas said.

"Well, that's the best you'll find. And trust me, I know, so don't bother questioning me on it. Would you want anything else, then? For yourself," the witch asked.

"I suppose I would," Thomas said, not wanting his visit to have been in vain.

"Come on back to the shack, then," she said. "Miranda, would you make sure he doesn't get lost? I don't want to walk." And she pulled one of her black shawls over herself, and was a crow again; and cawing she took flight for the branches above.

Miranda laughed and signaled for Thomas to follow her. "Don't tell me you're afraid of death?" she asked as he jogged to get in step beside her.

"I suppose I am," Thomas said. "But in all honesty I don't think about it much. What's your relation to the old woman?"

"I was born in the Hyacinth, too," she said. "The woods are still new to me, and I'm not sure I take to them. I'm stuffed with these colors – I miss the gray and white, in the winter." She reached behind Thomas' neck, and fondled the lowered hood of the mantle, caressing the blue crown with her fingers. "It's a pretty little thing, I suppose."

"Prettier than most," he said.

When they had made it back to the clearing, the witch had arrayed for Thomas a number of useful materials – ointments and herbs and things of that sort, to ease one's discomforts. Thomas took a promising flask from her, exchanging it for a small miscellany occupying his satchel that he didn't know the provenance or purpose of, and after that it was through the stump again, back into the winter, to follow the hazel home.

Thomas entered the quarters in the barony after dark. Rebekah was in the boy's room, sitting there by the workbench, turning an empty candlestick holder over in her fingers, and started when Thomas entered. "Where have you been?" she asked.

"Where have I been?" Thomas asked dully as he set his satchel on the bench. "I had an errand to run – materials for the boy."

"I didn't know where you were," Rebekah said. "I didn't know you weren't going to be here today."

"Oh?"

"It's just, you really ought to have told me, is all," Rebekah said, rising to leave. Thomas was blocking the doorway, so she stopped and waited for him to shuffle aside. As she moved past him, he laid his hand on her shoulder to stop her.

"You're right," he said. "I'm sorry. I'll make sure I tell you next time."

VIII

The next day Thomas rubbed the flying ointment on himself, and tucked in the space beneath his workbench, went out of his mind. He had been sitting there doing nothing, his eyes bulging open and his mouth set firm, listening to Rebekah and Eudoxia's muffled voices from the spinning room. This was too much, and visions came to him of being with her and the boy, of her talking to him like that for years to come, and of Thomas, Rebekah, and the boy eating at the little table in the quarters together. Each moment was one less until the time was up, and his ribs were constricting his heart. When he heard Rebekah laugh he gave in, reached up to the bench above, and unstoppered the flask.

The jimson weed's madness was vivid that day, and pleasant in its macabre way. Where a man flies as the temptation takes him is his business, and what Thomas saw came from his past, and perhaps the past of the whole Jasmine, all the slash-and-burn and slash-and-burn again. He flew to places far away, and now alighted with his jitters and tears spent, he sat in that most pleasant of clear states, in which the world had not quite returned to bother him, but the fancies were no threat anymore.

But where will I go? Where will I go? Thomas mused in his ease. Anyway, away from here – out of the barony, beyond the Hellebore, off the whole island. I hear the cry of the falcon, with golden wings to take me away, on up even out of the firmament, and I'll kiss the sky beneath my feet, and have dinner on God's chariot of glass and rainbows and lightning, next to his sapphires and four-headed pets.

He laughed, and said half-aloud in his drowsiness, "But why not? I'll go to the astral plane." It was no great trick to get there, and he'd long ago gotten the knack. There was never much call to bother with that place, but now he was infected with a fey triviality, and as he held his breath the question rang through him again – why not? He would try anything now, and that place was at least somewhere other than here. He shut his eyes, and laxed his muscles in that way that made his feet tingle, and he peered through the blackness, looking not at it but behind it, until his surroundings were stripped off him, and he was there.

The astral plane was much like the world, though dressed in cleaner colors. The day shone perpetually there, out of the unmoving yellow circle in the cloudless expanse of solid blue. Where the light met the blocks and cylinders strewn about the plane on which Thomas rested, it cast shadows as if calculated by a mason with a straightedge, the heat split cleanly from the shade. Those shadows formed a part of the ground, keeping always where they were, in the same shapes and at the same angles.

Thomas was still in the baron's estate, as the astral plane and the world shared their outline – wherever there was something of note there, so there was here, sketched in lonely, precise strokes. The frame of the building was brown, and the wood of the walls held only a single repeating pattern in the grain, too perfect in detail and belonging to no tree in particular. There was no roof, so that everything was perpetually open to the air, and in that air hung a near-perfect silence, troubled only by the faintest whine, like tinnitus, if one sat still for too long or strained to listen.

In the room with the boy, there was no boy – no one else was ever on the astral plane, not even fellow-travelers. The bed lay empty, nothing but a blocky frame whose material fused with the floorboards, and above it the parody of a mattress, like a slab of sculptor's marble with rounded corners. Thomas rose and placed his hand on it: though soft, it was unyielding to the touch. It disturbed him, to see that bed vacant, and it struck him suddenly that the baron's son was most likely a good kid.

There was nothing else on the floor, not even dust, though something like his workbench jutted from the wall, and his wizardly materials were spilt all over it, now a mess of oblong glass beads. He picked one of these up and peered through it, rolled it about his palm, and wondering whether he ought to pocket it, laughed with the dregs of the drug in him, and swallowed it instead – gulp the gewgaw, gewgaw's gone, his bleary thoughts hammered at him. At once he thought he should not have done this. It was as if the owner of the home might return at any second to find him out – the one that owned not just this second estate, but all the astral expanse.

His unease forced him away from the evil eye, and he left that place, passing by Rebekah's sparse spinning room and over the threshold of the cabin door. The elms in the paradise were unmarked gray cylinders without texture or branches, and the ground beneath them a flat, solid white. He left the enclosure: the frames of the buildings of the estate stood where they always did, and the ground was littered with a miscellany of featureless shapes, cones and cubes and spheres, all without blemish and big as cows, sunk partway into the earth or toppled on their sides, or standing pristine alone, or stacked one on top of the other.

He wound his way around these, and past the plot of tulips, perfect purple cups on straight green stalks, all evenly spaced and of a height. He tramped over the astral grass, which now covered the flat ground from horizon to horizon, a sea of green worms dancing and squirming as the fancy seemed to take them, ghostly pale and shining from within. They reached towards Thomas' boots as he approached them, seeming to yearn for his soles, but they could not detach themselves from their roots, so that the earth warped about him as he walked, leaning to caress him, but never reaching past his feet.

He found the courtyard, and the cherry tree was there, cast in finer detail than its surroundings, so that it was almost as it should be. He picked the fruit, which was always in season here, and it disintegrated in his hand to appear once again on the stem. The mockingbirds slept in the branches, and they never woke, even as Thomas poked their sides to rile them, and try as he might he could not pry them from their resting places.

Standing by the trunk and scowling at the cherries and the birds, again he felt the question, and with new intensity – why not? And to his surprise he felt anger, years dormant yet fresh now again, from the springs, as it was in his childhood. He asked the question as if to that unwavering tree, and a fearsome sobriety was coming on him, to sharpen his accusation. In the Jasmine, his kinsmen had refused to defend themselves, but he had told his attackers he would be of use to them, and lived. In the forest, the wizard had refused to flee with him, no matter the warnings he gave him, and Thomas had abandoned that man for whom he had such a fondness. He was there when Thomas returned, the bloody mantle of colors still on his back.

Could I not bring a man back to life? Thomas thought. Well, and why not? Am I any dumber than Elijah? How many times have I seen the strings that hold a man together being severed? How many men have I killed myself? Am I to believe that it all goes so easy one way, and not the other? And how many ways can they be unwound, that I cannot see even one to wind them together again? It had to happen at one time for us all to be born, so why not once more? And why not by me? And as he thought all this it seemed to him he heard laughter, deep and rumbling.

Then a thrill came over him, like the resolve to leap off a cliff into freezing water, or to go for the swipe when out picking pockets. It shot through his stomach and up to his head, where it had to escape, and he fell into a fit of sneezing. He sneezed three times, and four, and seven. He sneezed so hard that his frame rocked, and left him stunned; his muscles ached on his bones, and his vision went funny. He doubled over sneezing, and his throat and nose were racked with spasms.

And then he reared back his head with his mouth open one last time, and nothing happened. He exhaled, and inhaled again, listening to his own gentle breath, and the crinkle of the astral grass against his feet as he shifted them back and forth. He opened his eyes, and blinked, and everything was as it had been before: the bare sky, the breezeless air, and the featureless calm in a field of shapes. He waited for the cramps in his midsection to withdraw, and when he was sure the sneezes weren't returning, he stood upright, the spell off him. Saint Rock and his dog, Thomas thought, rubbing his nose. The pollen that must be in this place, or some joker brownie – like I was about to hack my wits up out of me.

And then he saw that everything was not as it had been. A fine mist limned the cherry tree, streaming off of it in excess like cold vapor off of ice. He rubbed his eyes, trying to make that mist disappear, but it would not; he reached out to touch it, it passed clean through his hand, and he felt nothing. It was the color of the light within the astral grass; he looked down at those blind worms, still caressing his feet, moving to feel and appease him, and worried that he had stayed too long. He was out of place here, and did not belong – someone was coming, and all at once he felt himself exposed in that wide open courtyard where the air whined at the edge of hearing. In a moment of panic he shut his eyes again, tensed his muscles, and retreated back through the blackness, until there he was.

Thomas sat on the floor, and the boy was there in the bed before him. He rose and had to rub his eyes again, to make sure: out of the center of the boy's chest, just above his doublet, the green mist was escaping. Like the mouth of a boiling kettle his body released the stuff, and it shot upward until it hit against the pale boundary of the dome and dispersed, then to fall into his body again. Thomas marveled, again wanting nothing more than to touch the vapor – and now he did, and it felt cool against his fingers, and curled itself about his hand on its way up.

He cupped his hands together and tried to cover the mist; it couldn't pass through him, and pooled together beneath his palms before finding its way around them. Gingerly he lowered his hands, keeping them in the way of the mist and approaching the invisible hole in the boy's chest. It was having difficulty escaping now, and with a jolt of courage he pushed all the way down, pressing his palms right against the chest at the source, so that nothing escaped at all. He stood there for several moments, breathing hard, his hands on the boy, and when he removed them, there was no mist left.

The pallor left the boy, and the flush came back to his cheeks, and his breath resumed, deep and even. He lay on the bed asleep, as if nothing had ever befallen him.

"Rebekah!" Thomas called in disbelief. He heard her mutter something to Eudoxia, and there was a shuffling of feet. "What is it, Dio?" he heard from behind him, and Thomas turned around to see Rebekah with her hands clamped over her mouth, her chest heaving up and down. "Oh, oh!" she shouted, and letting loose a wail of weird bereaved joy, she barreled out of the quarters, shouting the news to anyone who would hear her as she ran, and leaving Eudoxia looking after her, bewildered in her wake.

IX

It was the same man that had summoned Thomas past the gatehouse of the inner wall that led him now deeper into the heart of the Hellebore. In the shadow of the motte, he awaited the drawbridge, and followed after the baron's captain of the guard, up: up over the ditch and past the innermost wall, up past the tiny way-station on the hillside, where a lone man on a raised wooden platform waved them past, and up the stairs to the arched entrance of the stone keep, to gaze up at its five buttresses arrayed about the central tower, and the stark black flag flying from the parapet of each. Further up and further in, Thomas kept his eyes fixed on the bobbing tassel off the point of the guard's spear as he walked.

Within the keep, several flights of a spiral staircase along the gray walls took Thomas and his escort to a landing, and then into an antechamber that guarded the keep's center. The chamberlain waited there, seated behind a podium beside a rack of scrolls, like a cherub watching the passage to the master; even now, the baron had not descended from his sanctum. The chamberlain acknowledged Thomas as he shuffled in with the guard – if there was any contempt left in him, it was gone from his face. He nodded to allow the two of them to pass.

The guard pressed open the double doors, which gently resisted him with their weight, and shepherded Thomas within; leaving the entry open, he stood off to the left, planting his feet and the butt of his spear deliberately, and allowed Thomas to take in the administrative quarters of the baron. The slim romanesque windows left the chamber dim, but hung on the far wall could be seen a pennant, woven with the unmistakable colors of the Hellebore: five black petals arrayed about a yellow center, like the sun, all blooming out of the extended tongue of a snarling lion's head in profile.

In the middle of the room, seated behind a great desk of dark cherry wood, was the man Thomas had come to see. The shafts of afternoon light fell directly in front of him, so that the man was obscured while the work before him lay visible. Illumined there was another world, of ink and parchment, maps and missives. At the guard's signal, Thomas approached, and sat himself with uneasy gingerness in the chair placed before that desk. It creaked beneath his weight, and he let his sight adjust to see the baron.

The man's black, knowing eyes had an uncomfortable swiftness to them, and the way they darted across his work made plain that his hands were too sluggish to keep pace with the dictation of his mind. The blackness of those eyes had seeped into the pouches of skin below them, so that he appeared sleepless to the point of bruising. His eyebrows curled up and away from the dark below them, climbing his forehead in fear, and his hairline retreated up his skull in turn, to make way for their flight. He had the visage of horned owl – this man, Thomas thought, whose mind was too young for his body, though it was hard to tell the age of either.

The precise jerks and flourishes of his right hand stilled mid-character, and he let his quill hang above the page it scratched. The baron took a moment before darting his eyes up to meet Thomas'. The angle of his head was unchanged, still pointed toward the parchment, as if he could not leave off fully the thought tying him to it and animating his writing hand. And so his curled brows protected his gaze as he addressed Thomas. "Wizard," he said.

"Yes."

"I would like–" Thomas waited for the baron to regain his composure. "I would like for you to name a reward."

Thomas kept his eyes forward and spoke purposefully, wary not to entrap himself. "I agreed on a price with your chamberlain," he said.

"But I didn't earnestly think that you would bring my boy back to me."

"That is understandable," Thomas said.

"And he is worth more to me than – whatever that figure was."

Thomas' pulse was getting out of hand, and the blood made him sick. His hopes were taking shape within him. He had to restrain them, as they threatened to rise from his stomach and spill out of his mouth. In the baron's statement there returned to him a lifetime in miniature: the hunger and the ache, and the rain, and his dead brothers, and the line of soldiers winding down the valley by the Jasmine with smoke behind them, and the escape, and the dead wizard in the forest, on the day he took up the mantle. How banal his suffering was, how stupid all of life's trials, that moved the man without requiring or creating character – and he asked himself if this was it, and if at long last it was all over. Don't actually hope it, he told himself, or God might notice, and snatch it away; think nothing, but move your mouth and say the right words. Thomas speaks, but he is not here.

"If my lord is offering," Thomas said, "there is something I'd ask. On my way to the barony, I passed the tower down by the ford over the Cherrythorpe. I would like to be positioned with the wizards there, and given a post where I won't be bothered."

"Fine, it's done," the baron said, with the air of a man long accustomed to making decisions quickly, so that it no longer occurred to him to question his competence to do so. "Come back next Sabbath, and I'll have the documents ready, with someone to escort you. You may stay on here in the meantime, or not." He put his gaze back towards the desk, and the writing resumed. After a few moments, Thomas heard the guard approach from behind, and realizing that the audience was over, he stood. He hesitated, and placed his fingers gently on the finished cherry wood, so dark that the grain was obscured.

"And, if I might request one more thing of my lord –" Thomas said. The baron looked up from his parchment in polite expectation. "I would prefer, to the extent possible, that it were not known I can do this thing."

The baron puzzled over him, and was taken by a slow, faint sympathy. "Yes, as you say, then. And I ask you to reciprocate. The boy never died. The dead can't come back to life, of course."

"No," Thomas said. "They can't."

The baron smiled perfunctorily.

"I never had the chance to make the boy's acquaintance," Thomas said.

"I'm afraid you can't see him," the baron said. "He ought not know what happened to him."

The guard escorted Thomas back to the doors. Past the threshold, the man caught his attention. "Thank you, wizard," he said, "for what you did."

"Ah," Thomas said. "No problem."

Thomas went out of the antechamber, down and out: down the twisting stairs, out of the keep, down past the innermost wall and out of the bailey. He walked the path into town slowly, looking at his feet and the heather, and found his way to an alcove cut into the side of the church. He sat on the bench there, with his elbows on his knees; the gargoyle faces etched into the stone of the recession peeked at the corners of his vision.

There his genius came to him again, still as a painted bunting– a blue crown, red breast, and green wings, with the hues all bled together – and now with a jester's marotte tucked in the crook of its wing. The stick had perched on its tip a chunk of marble in the shape of Thomas' head, colored and detailed with unsettling precision, save for the eyes, which were wholly white, without iris or pupil. The bunting looked into Thomas' own eyes, and chirped a bright fanfare. It then began to strut left and right before his feet, in time with its own melody, bobbing its neck and pivoting to change direction at the end of each phrase. Then leaving off the birdsong, it began to shout, in time with its steps:

"O Death, where is thy sting?
O Death, where is thy sting?"

The marotte rose and fell with the contour of the refrain. Back and forth and back again the bunting marched, stepping high and kicking its twiggy little legs out. Behind it there was a shimmering of colors, and a line of facsimiles of the genius appeared – identical painted buntings of a smaller size, all in single file, each chirping and stepping in rhythm, and each turning back and forth to follow the bird directly preceding it. The taunt went on with the combined volume of their voices.

Thomas' eyes blurred as he watched the procession – he needed to look away, and so cast his gaze upwards, seeking out the soft solace of the gray sky. He found it, peeking out over the roof of the wing of the church that faced him from his vantage down in the alcove.

He heard noise – the noise of untrained feet tramping over stone – and a boy came into view on that roof. He was facing away from Thomas, picking his way roughly over the shingles, dropping frequently on all fours to keep his balance, and panting hard as he tried to suppress his giggling. He scurried up the slope, and reaching the spot where the bell gable met the roof, stood unsteadily to his full height, extended his hands over his head, and hopped just slightly to throw his fingers over the ledge. Scrabbling at the wall of the gable to find purchase, he got his footing, and with a wild effort swung himself up into the opening. Laughing and crouching, he ducked himself behind the body of the bell. He stayed still a moment, panting hard, and then peeked out from behind his perch, maneuvering his head carefully around the the bell, to look out at the town below him.

Thomas watched the back of the boy, who could not have been older than nine, for a minute as he stayed in this position and surveyed the ground. Over the buntings' singing he heard an avalanche of children's steps as they swept through the streets, out beyond the wing of the church that blocked Thomas' view. It was a game, and the boy was hiding from them, taken in by his own cleverness – until, Thomas told himself, one of the others thought to look at the roof from the opposite side. For a minute, nothing much changed, and Thomas pondered over the boy's mess of hair like straw behind the bell.

He then returned his gaze to the bunting, who was still marching, and still crying out its refrain with its procession of miniatures in step behind it. Back and forth it walked, and Thomas' eyes moved back and forth to match it. From above, Thomas heard the tramping of feet over stone once again, and the breathless giggling – it was time to find a new hiding spot. But then there was an abrupt clattering, and a yelp, and a thud. The bunting stopped in its tracks, and its miniatures evaporated – it looked to the ground beneath the bell gable, and Thomas followed, to see the boy lying on his back there, unmoving, unbreathing. He had played a bit too boldly; boys die for worse things, I suppose, thought Thomas.

He gazed at the boy's body for a while, as it spewed its life out of itself, and the bunting looked on as well in silence, its marotte and song forgotten. The fumes had the shape of a cone, whose definition dissipated as it drew away from the boy's body. The vapor sped forth hotly as it escaped his chest, and soon became confused, losing its conviction as it wandered farther into the open air, until it forgot that it existed and was not there anymore. The bunting seemed to have nothing to say to that. But after a few moments more, the bird turned to face Thomas, and pointed its free wing towards the boy laying there in the dirt, and chirped brightly before disappearing in its customary haze of light: red, blue, green.

Thomas sighed and pulled himself up off the bench. He darted glances to the left and to the right, to make certain no one was in eyeshot of him, and that no one had seen the boy's fall. When he was confident of his safety, he strode forward to position himself over the boy, and holding his breath he knelt to his chest. It was easier this time: his cupped hands captured the smoke, and sent it back to its origin, and when he leaned back from the boy's chest, the leak had been cauterized. Thomas stood again, his hands on his hips, curling his toes against the soles of his boots and watching the boy with taut nerves.

In just a few moments, it happened – the boy's breath returned to him, and there was a small groan and intake of air as he awoke. He blinked and squinted, and noticed that Thomas was there, leaning over him. He propped himself up on his elbows. Thomas offered the boy his arm, and pulled him to his feet.

"You took a tumble off the roof there," Thomas said.

"Oh," the boy said.

"Are you okay? You're not hurt?"

The boy was brushing himself off furiously and running his fingers through his hair. "I'm alright. Thanks, mister."

"You be careful, now, hey? You'll crack your neck doing that."

"Okay." And the boy, still covered in dust, ran off.

X

And so Thomas was taken up to the tower by the ford over the Cherrythorpe, some miles downstream of the town of the same name, and just before the first fork, where the banks light up in white in the spring. He knew that the wizards would sense nepotism in the baron's order, and that his foolishness would only confirm their suspicions – yet he felt only relief when the brothers took him in, and at his chrism he took Thomas as his name.

The tower had stood for a long time in disrepair, and pieces of its broken masonry lay strewn about the meadow on the river's edge, weather-stained and overgrown with daisies. Each of these stones, and each of those still in the tower on up to the crenellations, was marked with little symbols that Thomas couldn't decipher, and in the hours between his work he went to the roof to look out over the country, trying to match the shape of the marks to the things he saw below him. In time he grew accustomed to the brothers, and the goat pen and orchard and all the iridescent little orbs that floated amiably about the tower grounds, and his worry left him.

The brothers came and went from the tower as they needed to or as it pleased them, and they mostly slept in the open, so that it was often uncertain where they were. And while the townspeople in the Cherrythorpe worked hard each day, and did nothing on the Sabbath, the wizards worked too on the Sabbath, but did not work hard each day. When Thomas asked Polycarp the abbot about this odd habit, Polycarp answered him, "We don't work on the Sabbath – we're always at rest. We may move about and do our tasks then, but that isn't work. In fact, we never work at all. So we keep the Sabbath better than anyone. It's the whole week, for us."

And so the unending Sabbath passed for Thomas in slow cycles, with all its menial tasks, magical and mundane. He made excuses when he was unable to change the wind or do the light show, and in time his cover became too plain, and he knew that no one could seriously think he was a practitioner of magic like them. Yet in doing the motions, the power accreted on him, until he could not distinguish himself from his brothers, and he was a wizard in truth. And no one ever mentioned it to him.

At the tower they brewed beer and grew vegetables that tasted a bit better than elsewhere, mended cracked ribs, and blasted hunks of rock into sculpture. He came to understand that wizards did not actually make use of magic all that often, and less so the more they came to know, so that the difference between a wizard and an ordinary man became less apparent, the further apart they were. At length Thomas allowed the rain to fall on him, rather than warding it away, and in time there were days when he scarcely moved at all.

He watched the clouds drift from one end of the sky to the other, and waited for his own fingernails to grow, and in that torpor he learned a number of things. He learned, for instance, that rabbits have souls – not just fears and sensibilities, which is plain enough to anyone, but mythologies, and lives in the shape of sagas, in which they aspire and fail. He learned as well that he was not one man, but a chain of men, one behind another. When he grew hungry he once thought, "I'm hungry," but then he came to think "Thomas is hungry," and it was he who noticed this about Thomas. So his hunger was both his own and not his own, and it did not motivate him of its own accord, but only offered something to that second man behind Thomas, for his consideration. And behind this second man was a third, and on and on.

"Do you know, brother Thomas," brother Bartholomew asked him one day as they sat out in the garden during the autumn chill, "what is up *there*, out by the welkin, between heaven and earth?"

"I don't know," Thomas said.

"Nothing," brother Bartholomew said. "If you were to go up, and up, and up – you would never hit anything. The air would get nastier, and harder to breathe, and colder, until there would be nothing left. And it would all just happen by subtle shades: there would be no landmark to divide your passage from one realm to the other, no barrier to stop you from going any which way, and nothing of any interest. Miles and miles in every direction, there would be nothing at all."

Out in the country, wandering and on call, Thomas saw more than he ever had on the farm in the Jasmine or during the war, though he never ventured more than a week's walk from the tower. There was a landscape there now, not just a network of indistinct hostile passageways between water and civilization, and the holy sites and towns had no particular claim on him. The tower's domain was older than the fiefs, and so cut indiscriminately through the Cherrythorpe, the Hellebore, and several direct holdings of the crown where no one lived but the wizards and varmints. The signposts could be ignored; every piece of that land was as richly contoured as every other, yet never with the same shapes.

He slept for some nights by a pond south of the tower, and on the waking days in between kept watch over it, puzzling over the tadpoles and arrowheads. But his attention turned soon to the stones ringing the water, and to one in particular, stained with slime on the wet side. He looked it over, and over again, studied the border between the green and the gray, and counted all the little flecks in its surface. He thought he was looking at a country, and became familiar with its topography, which may as well have been criss-crossed by roads and dotted with fine little castles. Or perhaps it was not a country, but a world: the bump on the rock's dry side was the cosmic mountain, and the pond was the cosmic ocean. And on that mountain was a grain of sand, in which all that structure was repeated again. No place was really larger than any other: they were all of them infinite.

Thomas learned that this infinity was found even in nothing at all. He had taken to closing his eyes more often, and he noticed that, contrary to what he had always taken for granted, it was not all dark behind his eyelids. The lights that bled in and out of his vision in the void at first seemed barely there at all, just disturbances in the blank texture without distinct shape or hue. But as he turned them over they leapt forward and back, and swirled and encompassed one another, in turquoise and orange and yellow, and colors he had never quite seen. They were so subtle, so ephemeral, that around their edges he sometimes could not tell whether he imagined them, and soon his little turns of mind shaped them into unending prismatic landscapes, with nuckelavees rearing out of the mist. He made gods, and palaces that they wiped away with wrathful storms.

"For what is your life?
For what is your life?"

He asked this, while watching the phosphenes, to the creatures in the back of his eyes.

Thomas went without complaint where Polycarp sent him, unshod and carrying a staff and satchel. It was people more often than the wilds that called for a wizard: there would be a blindness to exorcize, a broken rain-catcher, or a rash of infertility in the quails. Some problems he was able to fix, in a few minutes' time or in a week's, and for others he left the people with his apologies, and a trinket and a blessing for their consolation. They would sometimes feed him for his trouble, and this was the only meat he ever had – he didn't know whether he was allowed to eat it, but he did. More than once he suspected that in the past he'd ransacked a village he now served, but if it were possible for anyone to recognize him, they did not behind his mantle and beard.

Several years on, a party led by the baron took passage to a political summit at the Quarryman's fort, and on the way made the tower at the Cherrythorpe their caravanserai. They pitched their tents at the ford that night, in preparation to cross next dawn. The baron himself, among the officers who took what empty tower rooms were available, asked the abbot whether brother Thomas happened to be around. Polycarp affirmed that he was, and set a flare up in the sky to recall him from the woods a mile away.

Thomas was sitting on the pallet in his cell, whittling a protective charm in the likeness of a fishhook, when the baron entered to see him. The room was open to the sky and to a drop of thirty feet to the grass and stones below, owing to a massive hole in its out-facing wall, and Thomas was flinging the wood shavings out into the twilight. Without rising or taking his eyes off his work, he said, "My lord."

The baron hesitated for a moment before sitting in the cell's only chair, in front of a rude table. Neither of them spoke for a minute or so, and the soft sound of Thomas' knife went on. When at length he stopped and looked the baron in the face, he saw that the man's right eyelid had begun to droop since he'd seen him last. "I owe a lot to you," Thomas said.

"It's funny," the baron said. "Though I saw you only for a moment, in the Hellebore, I felt that I ought to contrive to see you again, from the moment I learned we'd be passing up Cherrythorpe way."

"Thanks," Thomas said. "Your presence dignifies me." He returned to his whittling.

"It's just that, you understand," the baron said. "I tend to think of you when I think of my son. I started to wonder, absurdly, if you had been real."

"Yes," Thomas said. "And how is your son?"

"He's dead," the baron said.

Thomas flushed, and his hands stopped working. "But how can it be?"

"It didn't have to do with your handiwork. A fever took him three years later."

"But my lord, why not send for me? I have been here."

"It would have been too painful to lose the same child three times," the baron said. "I judged it better just to have another."

Thomas set down the wood and the knife and rose to fetch some alcohol from the cellars. He returned with this and a second chair, sat with the baron, and spoke to him about dying, and things of that nature.

In the grip of the spirits and candlelight, he told him plainly all that he hadn't before: who he was, and what he had done prior to coming to the Hellebore, and where he had learned his first magic tricks, and by what means he had gotten the mantle. He told him about the men that killed his brothers in front of him in the Jasmine, and then took him along. Thomas told the baron everything, save for how he came upon the secret of life and death – that he reserved, and passed over in silence. And the baron told Thomas of his own bastardy, and that Rebekah had a boy: not Thomas', not the baron's.

That was the last time he saw the baron, and Thomas lived there, at the tower by the ford over the Cherrythorpe, until he seized up in his middle age, and he was buried out in the graveyard with the rabbits, and his body stiffened, and bloated, and crawled with maggots, and decayed. And when the baron heard of this, he recalled his distant sympathy, and unable to draw himself away from that man, commissioned the epitaph of his tombstone, and it said:

Brother THOMAS
Who was a wizard
And committed crimes in the king Jordan's war
And conquered death,
bringing back to life John the son of the baron in the Hellebore

Acknowledgments

Thanks to: my mother Victoria and brother Matthew, who read earlier drafts and chapters of this story and offered line-editing and broader comments and suggestions; my friends Cameron and Josef, who read things I wrote, including earlier, worse fantasies; my Aunt Peggy, who read *The Hobbit* to me as a kid; Mark and Dennis, for agreeing to publish this, for suggestions and editing, and the cover art.

About the Author

Patrick grew up on the border of Los Angeles and San Bernardino counties, in a regular suburb, and then a nice one. He went to school in San Diego, worked as a linguist in Chicago, then gave that up and came back to California to live in the San Diego area, working in a public library and then for Meals on Wheels in North County. He currently lives in the poorest zip code in Vista, and in addition to all the book and language stuff, likes theology, music, and hiking. This is his first non-academic publication.

112 N. Harvard Ave. #65
Claremont, CA 91711

chapbooks@bamboodartpress.com
www.bamboodartpress.com